SAM SWALLOW
AND THE
RIDDLEWORLD LEAGUE

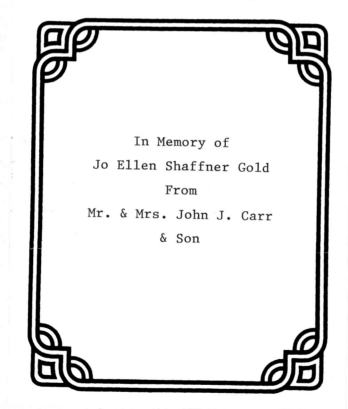

In Memory of
Jo Ellen Shaffner Gold
From
Mr. & Mrs. John J. Carr
& Son

Book design by Elisa Gutiérrez

Printed in Canada in October 2013 by Sunrise Printing, Vancouver, BC.

LIBRARY AND ARCHIVES CANADA CATALOGUING IN PUBLICATION

New, W. H. (William Herbert), 1938-, author
    Sam Swallow and the riddleworld league / by William New
; illustrations by Yayo.

ISBN 978-1-896580-98-2 (pbk.)

    I. Yayo, illustrator II. Title.

PS8577.E776S36 2013   jC811'.54   C2013-902657-6
. . . .

The publisher wishes to thank João Simas Ferraz for his editorial assistance.

The publisher thanks the Government of Canada and Canadian Heritage for their financial support through the Canada Council for the Arts, the Canada Book Fund and Livres Canada Books. The publisher also thanks the Government of the Province of British Columbia for the financial support it has given through the Book Publishing Tax Credit program and the British Columbia Arts Council.

 **Canada Council
for the Arts** **Conseil des Arts
du Canada** BRITISH
COLUMBIA
ARTS COUNCIL

WILLIAM NEW

SAM SWALLOW
AND THE
RIDDLEWORLD LEAGUE

♦ ILLUSTRATIONS BY YAYO ♦

Tradewind Books
VANCOUVER · LONDON

*For Frank—*Y

*This book is for every child who loves
the games that words can play—*WN

C O N T E N T S

CHAPTER 1

◆

The House at the End of the Tram Line

Sam was bouncing. All over the house, all over the yard—TODAY WAS THE DAY!

He was so excited—and yet so On Edge—that he'd already knocked over at least Ten Important Things inside the house, including a pitcher of sunflowers. His father had sent him outside, shouting "SAMMY! NO CRASHING!"

Small chance of that.

Sam had hours to fill before he could go try out for the baseball team, and he couldn't just do nothing. So he climbed on top of the shed, bellowed "MY NAME'S SAM" at anyone in earshot, leaped over the lettuce patch, stood on his head and looked at the world upside down. Later on he figured out an anagram for NO CRASHING—CHIN GROANS.

Sam loved word puzzles. Before long he'd thought of at least two anagrams for TODAY'S THE DAY—

> TIDY TOADS, YEAH,
>
> IT'S TOAD HEYDAY,

and another for SAM BELLOWS LOUD—
OWL SLAMS DOUBLE,
and said to himself, *They all sound Great!* Then he ran around the garden, playing chase with his pet cat Clio.

"Clio," Sam's Uncle Donovan once said, "That's an a-mews-ing name." Sam laughed at the pun, and at Clio, who kept jumping away from the unpredictable sprinkler Sam's dad had hooked up to an outside faucet.

Mostly Clio just lurked in the bushes, and pounced on soccer balls, or catnip mice, or whatever hopped by. Though Sam saw her catch a sparrow once—not something he liked remembering.

• • •

By ten o'clock Sam had gone in and out the back door at least a hundred times, looking for a tennis ball and a catcher's mitt. He'd been told not to slam the door, ten times, for sure. But the screen door at the back of their house just sort of slammed on its own.

Didn't it.

Whenever anyone went in or out.

Besides, his father said every week he was going to fix that door and find the key to the one at the front, and he never did. He never had the time, he always said.

And anyway, TODAY WAS THE DAY—Sam was Ten Years Old, and today he was determined to try out for the baseball team at Byrd City Park. Which is why he was outside now, in his blue-and-gold shirt, the colour of his favourite baseball team, practising catching—bouncing a tennis ball off the side of the house and catching it when it rebounded—Bam!

Sam tried to be quiet, but you could hear the noise everywhere in the house and, throwing the ball again, he wondered if people could hear him maybe even a whole kilometre away (1093.61 yards—Sam was good at numbers. He knew how far it was between bases: 60 feet. Or 18.288 metres—he'd learned metric conversion too). Then he flinched as he lost his concentration and dropped the ball.

BAM! he threw it harder, impatient with himself, impatient to be off to the park. And BAM! threw it again, wanting to keep on practising, just in case it helped—practise even on his own, today of all days—

On his own because this morning no one had had time to play catch. "No time today, sport," his father had said.

"Ask Cory," his mother had said. "He'll play with you. Or Ann will."

But no such luck. His brother and sister were busy—Cory off to play basketball, Annie to practise diving and swimming. "Sorry," they both said. "Maybe tomorrow?"

Even Uncle Donovan wasn't willing to play today—though he often wrestled with Sam, threatening to turn him into a pretzel. Or showed him magic tricks, chanted crazy rhymes, and told stories about explorers caught in the ice and giant birds that picked people up and carried them off to their secret lair. Sometimes he glared fiercely and added "even pterodactyls (that means 'wing-fingers,' Sammy)."

On a good day, Sam laughed with him, but today Uncle Donovan just said "No." Croaked "no" was more like it. He'd come down with a bad cold and had lost his voice. *He's being really crabby*, Sam thought. Almost as annoying as the kids at school, the ones who kept teasing him, telling him he was too short to join the team. *It isn't their team, even if they say it is.*

His last name made everything worse. *Swallow.*
Face it.
I'm Sam Swallow.
In Byrd City.

Yes, he knew that Byrd City was named for Admiral Byrd, the great explorer—he'd been told it over and over—"that's why that big bronze statue stands in the centre of town." "Neat," Sam always answered. But who cares about a statue with an owl always perched on the top of its head? Not Sam. Not when he had to deal with catcalls on the playground.

The Weaver twins were especially annoying. They kept asking him to fly.

It's not funny.

Sam ignored the Weaver twins whenever they teased him like that to get his attention. Most of the time. Occasionally he'd think of throwing one of his Uncle Donovan's weird rhymes back at them.

Donovan Donovan Sullivan Blake
Call me a name and your belly will ache

But rhymes never solved anything. So usually Sam just laughed the teasing off and went back to whatever he was doing. Maybe a number puzzle. He just wished everything was different, that's all.

And he really didn't like being called Sammy. *It's a little kid's name.*

OK, he was short—he knew that—but he wasn't little, and his name was Sam, not Sammy, though that's the name his father called him by. Others too. Even Parker their parrot kept repeating SamMEE, SamMEE. Over and over.

But then Sam remembered how Cory and Annie argued with each other—who was smarter, who could hold their breath longer, "I can," "Can not," "Can too," "No way," "Way"—and figured, *no one's right all the time.*

The kids at school, for instance. When they told Sam he couldn't play baseball, that wasn't true at all. He could catch really well. He knew that. And run as fast as the rest of them, too. As for batting a ball, and pitching, and fielding—well, he was learning. Cory showed him his special three-fingered pitch. His dad was always showing him how to swing a bat. And his sister Annie, who was 12, said things like "Focus—let everything else fall away, like water off a widgeon's back." *Whatever that meant.*

He just had to go to the Park and show everyone what he could do.

"Forget those other guys, Sam," Cory said. "Wear your name—be proud of who you are."

Easy for him to say, Sam thought. *He's 14. He's already tall. He's always eating. And he's not here.*

Nor is anyone else. They're all busy.

Maybe looking after Littlebird. Oliver. His little brother.

"Littlebird" was Annie's name for Oliver. She'd called him that right from the start, and everybody else just copied her.

Someone was usually looking after Littlebird—feeding him, reading him stories, rocking him to sleep, singing him that kookaburra lullaby they always sang.

Well, maybe right now they were doing something else. Didn't matter.

Uncle Donovan, though—Sam knew for sure what Uncle Donovan was doing. He was hovering over a crossword puzzle, being grumpy.

BAM!

I have to get on a team, Sam told himself, throwing the ball against the house again—*Today!* **BAM!** and

BAM!—

till five minutes to twelve, when his mother called quietly from the screen door, "Sammy, come in for lunch. Please stop crashing the house, and please don't slam the door—you'll wake up Littlebird."

"Okay," Sam said, as he climbed the five steps from the yard to the deck. "And after lunch I'm going right to the park."

He was laughing as he pushed open the screen door and stepped inside—until he heard it SLAM! behind him.

"Sammy," his father was sharp-eyed and stern. "I've told you a thousand times: Stay In or Go Out, but Do Not Slam!"

"But," Sam started to say—

But Uncle Donovan interrupted, rasping, "Sammy, Control Yourself—or you'll—you'll—you'll turn into something I can't think of—" His throat choked up and his threat turned into a thunderous fit of raucous coughing.

He makes more noise than I do, Sam thought. *More noise than me and the door together.*

Annie was already sitting down at the kitchen table, her hair still wet from swimming. Clio the cat—curled up on an overstuffed armchair, perilously close to another pitcher of sunflowers—was opening one eye from time to time to stare at Parker the parrot, who kept squawking. "NO CRASHING, NO CRASHING!"

Clio ignored everyone else—until Cory stumbled back into the house, complaining loudly that he'd just bumped his head on the doorframe. Clio leaped from the chair then and slipped toward the back door, ready to dart underfoot when it next opened.

But Sam scarcely noticed. He was so excited he almost couldn't eat. Today was the day when his life was going to change—

Then suddenly he looked at the clock—five minutes to one ALREADY?

"I'll be late," he blurted, "the tryouts will be starting—"

"Better hop to it, then," his father said.

"You could take the tram," said his mother.

"Breathe deep," said his sister.

"See ya," said his brother.

Littlebird was nowhere to be seen.

The last thing Sam heard, as he and Clio rushed out the door, was his uncle's scratchy voice flapping, "Don't get yourself in such a twist—be free as a bird—but watch out for that cat or you'll answer to me."

Sam didn't see the raven flying low overhead, or the long shadow that the raven cast on the ground in front of him, or the eagle circling high above. Or the cat under his feet.

Nor did he pay attention to anything that might be in his way, like the ball that he'd left on the deck when he'd last come in to the house, and that anyone could easily have slipped on or skidded on or tripped over. Suddenly

flying? The deck upside down—
Or falling? The earth so close—
Slam.
And instantly
still.

Something curious and very un-ordinary had happened.

When the door slammed, it made no sound at all.

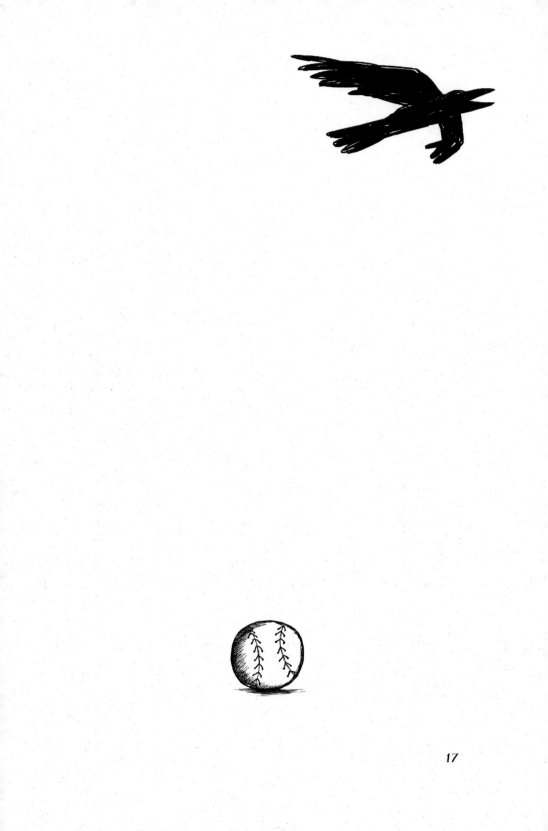

CHAPTER 2

◆

SIGNS AND SPLINTERS

In fact, the whole world had changed.

• • •

Sam looked around. No one there. No Cory, no Annie. No Uncle, no Oliver. Even the house had disappeared.

He listened closely. Nothing.

No one coughing or sneezing, complaining or teasing. No beep, no bleep, no buzz, no blare, no honk, no cronk, no anything there.

But—but—

When he looked down at his hands and feet, they weren't there either.

Sam was flabbergasted. He had no hands and feet. He'd—what? He'd grown wings and claws!

He brushed his face very carefully with a wing tip— and sneezed. He had a beak, not a nose! And instead of clothes—*what happened to my clothes?*— he had feathers: shiny blue on top, a dark orange throat, a pale chest, a forked tail. *A tail? He was the very size of a barn swallow!*

What's going on? he tried to shout. *I'm a BIRD?*

It didn't sound like a shout. More like a peep. Like being tongue-tied, as if he'd lost his voice.

Just then he heard—well—something. Something from nearby bushes that sounded a little like—*twittering? rhyming?* "Who's there?" he cheeped. "Clio?" *If it is, then she'd be bigger than me. That could be a problem.*

And if the sounds are supposed to be saying something, what is it? A twitter-rhyme?

It just sounded nonsensical:

If muddle befuddles, your trouble redoubles—
No grumbling, crumbling—Chortle instead—
You know where you're going, so why are you slowing—
The world is in tatters—unfetter your head—
Puzzles can muzzle, but riddles have middles—
Untangle the strangle and scramble ahead—

The twitter-rhyme echoed slightly, then drifted away.

I can't make head or tail of this. Sam tried to laugh—but it didn't sound funny.

He was sure of one thing, though. He had heard the word *riddle*. *Riddles have solutions—all I have to do is solve them. If everything's in tatters—who's telling me this?—I guess I have to put it all back together somehow. But how?*

Think, he told himself.

Sam craned his neck to look farther afield. *Where am I?* Where had his family's garden gone? Blades of crabgrass, almost as tall as he was, blocked his view. Pebbles as big as boulders, twigs as large as branches—everything around him looked enormous and strange. He was certain he'd just taken five steps across his back deck, but nothing he could see looked familiar. No sign of Clio. No mice. No toads. No anyone.

Who am I expecting? he snorted. *Penguins?*

He tried to shrug, but the feathers on the back of his neck scarcely moved.

So?

So what do I know for sure?

He knew where he'd been going—the park where the Byrd City baseball league played. *So I just have to find it, that's all. Easy.*

Or maybe not.

Though why should anything get in my way now? Nothing's stopped me before.

Turning around, he spied a sign lying in the grass. *A broken sign.* The sign looked as though some creature with claws had torn it to tatters, for all it said was

Looks sort of like a Laugh, thought Sam, *if you read it out loud.* A bunch of other letters lay scattered beside it—an A, an N, an R, two T s, and half of a W —Sam dismissed them.

Useless.

The moment he thought that, the splintered sign and all the letters evaporated.

Were they real?

Then he had an inspiration. *If I'm a bird, maybe I can take off!*

But can I? Fly?

Even walking was difficult. But flying?

Running and swinging two wings just didn't work. All Sam managed to do was make scratch marks on the ground and lose his balance. Soon his sense of direction deserted him as well.

Face it: I'm lost.

But I am still Sam—sort of. And I still want to try out for the baseball team.

Even if I do have feathers.

So I have to figure out what to do.

Maybe I can talk to other birds, if there are any, if I can find one, if I can get my voice back.

Maybe I can ask them how to get to the park.

Just then Sam saw a green-backed humming-bird and started to chase it. The hummingbird seemed to be humming Something. *Is it talking to me? Did it actually say*

Quickly   Me   Here

Follow   There

It was hard to tell. The bird words came in the wrong order. They lasted just a fragment of a millisecond before they flew off. And they sounded as though they were everywhere at once. *Or else nowhere.*

Never here.

Wherever here is.

Figuring out what cheeps and peeps mean is really hard. Chirps, too, and twitters and tweets and cackles and warbles and squawks. It's like trying to catch words in a butterfly net.

Determined, Sam kept moving through the grass to a crossroads where he'd last seen the humming-bird. Two pointed signs abruptly appeared on a post.

Help at last, thought Sam. But though he could read the signs clearly, they didn't seem to help much. They argued instead. *What? The signs are talking? I can hear them? Do I suddenly understand bird talk as well?*

One sign shouted:

◀ THERE'S A ROOSTER ON THE ROAD— WHICH WAY IS HE GOING, CROWING? ▶

The other shouted back:

▶ THERE'S A CROW ON THE ROAD— WHERE WILL HE ROOST? ◀

Sam looked at the first, then at the second. *Which way would Sam go?* he wondered. Then he whispered, "Why did I ask that? Aren't I still Sam?"

The lullaby that his parents used to sing ran through his head—

Do the kestrel and the condor hover,
Cutting out the light?
Don't worry little kookaburra.
Sleep—

Sam kicked the ground. He didn't sing along. "Even if I'd sung it, it wouldn't have helped make sense of what's going on," he muttered, slowly getting his voice back. *I'm not a kookaburra. I'm not little. I don't want to sleep. And I AM still Sam!*

"So, what are you going to do?" he asked himself, sounding a bit more like his father than he intended. "Hop to it—or just sit here and roost?"

♦

CHAPTER 3

OLD SWIVELHEAD'S ADVICE

All at once Sam heard a sharp, piercing cry. He looked to the left, then looked to the right. Then, looking directly over his head, he saw three owls standing on the signpost: one was striped, one was white, and one seemed to have horns.

I'm sure they weren't there a minute ago.

"Who do you think you are, young bird?" asked the middle owl. The white one, Sam was pretty sure. He could definitely understand what this bird was saying.

"Why are you here and why did you wake us up? It's the middle of the day. We're Night Owls—don't you know anything?"

"I'm Sammy—I mean Sam—Swallow," said Sam, swallowing.

"Well, which is it?"

"It's Sam," said Sam, a little more firmly. "I was on my way to play baseball in Byrd City Park, but I don't know how to get to the park because I don't know where I am. Where am I?" It was the longest he'd spoken in quite some time. Then a second question tumbled out: "And who are you?"

"Isn't it obvious?" asked the white owl. "We're the Three Owls. My name is Snow." She was clearly the most talkative of the three. Waving a wing at the owl beside her, she added, "And she's Bard. She always speaks in verse."

"I don't like verse," said Sam, thinking about Uncle Donovan's weird rhymes.

"Could be worse," said Snow, a little icily. "We could all talk in Wingdings, and then where would you be?"

👀■♎ ♦∿♏■ ♦∿♏□♏ ♦□♦●♎ ◈□♦
♌♏✍

"See what I mean?"

Bard turned, looked at Sam for a long moment, and then spoke, grumpily:

If you're averse to every rhyme,
You'll never reach the field on time—

To play on a team you have to laugh:
Would you rather pout in a paragraph?

So if yourself you choose to find,
Ten riddles here you must unwind—

Whatever else you say or see,
You must avoid Catastrophe.

I give you this advice for free:
Stay unannoyed. Be clear. Like me—

With that, Bard closed her eyes and went back to sleep.

"Clear?" snapped Sam. "I don't have any idea what you're saying! Where IS Here? Why does nothing make sense?"

"You're in Riddleworld, of course," replied Snow. "You asked to be different, and so different you are. The rhymes are telling you this. You just aren't listening. Here in Riddleworld nothing is obvious. Everything real is in disguise. Or upside down or backwards.

"When you think things don't matter, they appear to disappear—even though you might need them, and even if you ought to remember them. You'll hear helpful things and hurtful things. You just have to figure out which is which."

Snow was no easier to understand than Bard was.

"Owls come in all sizes," she added. "Tiny Elf to Great Grey Ghost. We Three are The Owls Who Guard the Signpost. We help travellers who deserve our help. When we can. A little Saw-whet Owl should be here, too. His name is Owlet. He sounds like a saw being sharpened, and he needs to be called back.

"Unfortunately, without Owlet with us we're not able to help. We can only offer clues. Old Swivelhead here decides what the clues will be. She's a Great Horned Owl."

Abruptly the old Horned Owl swivelled her head toward Sam, opened one eye, looked him up and down, and said in a very deep gruff voice, "I've been listening. I've not been asleep. And I've decided . . ."

"Please," said Sam.

"That's better," said Old Swivelhead.

"But how will I, how can I, where, when . . .? " began Sam.

"No Buts," she answered. "Just listen. I don't have all the time in the world."

 While Old Swivelhead was speaking, a rufous cuckoo landed on the signpost. The old owl asked her the time.

"Just enough," the cuckoo called out, "if he hops to it, hops to it."

She flew off. "Has to start soon—"

"I see," said the Great Horned Owl, cocking her head. "You have the ability to get where you want to go, but it is a long way away. Others have tried before you, and some end up just spinning in the dust, so focus. The park is at the extreme edge of Riddleworld, and the journey there will be hard. You will have to go through Riddle City. A splendid likeness of the Admirable Bird, the Great Surveyor, once stood there, but the Cats have been disrupting the city, ripping it apart. Watch out for the Claws. The path is dangerous.

"On the way, you'll have to deal with distractions of all kinds. Use your skill with numbers, cope with the Anagram Wall, and unriddle Ten Riddle-tasks. Are you ready for the challenge?"

"Yes," answered Sam, almost believing what he'd just said.

"These are your Riddle-tasks," Old Swivelhead continued. "You must:

1. compose the S and arrange the signs,
2. pass the time (and remember to rhyme),
3. enter the maze and escape it again,
4. call a tongue-untwister to break the chains,
5. sing a song that's known to Sam,

7. break the ice to catch the tram,
8. find a stream and cross it cleverly,
9. meet the Eagle, enjoy the revelry,
10. then count back from ten to one.
If you get this far, you'll think you're done."

"You left out Number 6," blurted Sam.

"So I did," replied the owl, fixing one eye on Sam for an extra-long minute.

Then she continued, "Along the way you must also:
6. rescue the One Who's Lost in the middle of Riddleworld."

Sam took a deep breath.

Old Swivelhead kept talking. "You will need two friends. One will be a Careful Giant and the other will be a Smallbird with brains. They will have skills that can help you. And you must also help them. Everything's a riddle here. Whenever you think you are done, there will still be more to do."

"I don't have any friends," mumbled Sam. "Not here, anyway. And where will I find the maze? And I don't know what a tongue-untwister is."

"Speak clearly," said the Owl.

"Who is the One Who's Lost?"

"*Listen*. And look carefully. *Somehow letters* will reveal him to you. If you could *grow lettuce*, you could see him. *Swallow etiquette* will take you to him. Cross *yellow lines* if you would seek him. *Narrow-leaved* vines will almost hold him. *Windowlight* will nearly reach him. *Stay on the ground* and you will miss him. *Rope and cage* do not contain him. He is hidden, and small, and I will *now let* you go."

Sam started to move but Old Swivelhead had more to say: "Although you might find it difficult to remember all these clues at once, a Burrowing Owl

will help you. He is camouflaged in *sunflowers*, because of the Cats. You might never see him. But along your way, you will remember more of the clues every time you think of *sunflowers*."

"But I NEVER think of sunflowers," Sam protested.

"Perhaps you will," replied the owl. "Or perhaps you won't. But if you do, pay careful attention. Because only if you follow the clues closely, solve the riddles correctly, and complete all your tasks will you find your field, play your game, and in the end 1 2 3 and a 4th reach home."

"That doesn't make sense," said Sam.

"This is Riddleworld, what do you expect?" hooted the old owl, who promptly swivelled away, folded up and went back to sleep, leaving Sam a little stunned and even more confused than he had been before.

Was that helpful or not? he wondered.

Maybe I can ask Snow and Bard to explain what Old Swivelhead means. But Bard would just tell me another riddle-rhyme.

"Snow?"

"If you get flummoxed, try moving ahead. If you need more help, try writing me a letter. But don't expect the clues to get any easier. Old Swivelhead's decision is final," said Snow.

Final, at least, was a word Sam understood.

If I don't try, I'll end up in the dust. So I'd better solve some riddles. That's what.

• • •

Sam decided then that he'd rather follow the ROOSTER sign than the CROW sign. *I want to go on, not to roost.* So he picked one of its two arrows and headed out along a white painted line at the shrubby edge of an open field.

The field looked like an abandoned scrub-lot where no one had played for many seasons. Instead of green grass: dry stubble. Instead of flowers: a random scatter of shattered pots, plastic fragments, chunks of old metal—rusty tins and bent nails and iron stakes and broken address numbers off old houses, splinters and chips, all covered in dust. *Some of them look a bit like talons and dried-out feathers.* He started to hurry. A broken notice board read

TH WEATHERVAN.

I think those are the same letters as the one on the
broken sign—I wonder what they're trying to say.

All at once Sam heard rustling in the shrubbery
alongside, and slowly the rustling began to sound
like the chatter of a lot of bird voices.

"The Swallow's here . . . he's seen the Owl . . . do the
Cats know? Is their fur on end? You have to hide when
the fur's on end . . . or the tail flicks . . . or the claws
come out . . . especially Klaw's."
"Shhh," said a louder voice. "Klaw will hear. The Raven
will tell him."

The birds started to talk of old stories they'd first
heard as chicks, especially one called *The Swallow*
and His Friends.

"Remember the Great Swallow?"
"Yes, he came out of nowhere in early spring, and
banished the winter-cats."
"With his friends," said another.
"I thought it was just a story," another whispered,
"about when the birds were happy."

Other voices joined in, all talking at once.

"When they trusted each other and played games . . .
before Klaw built his tower and the yowling Cats broke
the statues in Riddle City . . . especially the fine bronze
figure of the Admirable Bird."
"And don't forget Wing Commander Bird . . . Flight
Lieutenant Bird . . . Crow-Magnon Bird . . . before they
built Pterodactyl Fingerwing."
"Those long teeth . . . the terrible claws!"

What ARE they talking about?
A Raven? with Teeth? Sam glanced up at the sky.
Was something flapping? Not that I can see.
Suddenly he heard the voices say:

". . . that was before the Cats stole the One Who's Lost
in the middle of Riddleworld, and insisted that all the
Owls surrender—"

Sam froze in mid-stride. *That's something I need
to know.*

But just then a great fluster rustled the bushes
and new voices babbled,

"He's been seen . . . he's been seen . . . I heard the Cats hissing . . . 'Trespasser Swallow! He's out of control!'"
"They want to slow him down and fluster him, toy with him as though he's a catnip mouse . . . or a trivial toad."

Sam bristled, held his head higher, listened more intently.

"No time, no time. He has to be warned . . . the Cats will ensnarl him. They want the Raven to snatch him."

The voices stopped.
The Raven! Catch ME? Sam looked up again. *No Raven there.*
Nothing there.
Not yet anyway.
He hurried on, his claws scrabbling in the dust. He still didn't know where he was heading, but he knew for sure that he didn't want to stay put.
I wish I could fly.

CHAPTER 4

♦

CROSSWORD GARDENS

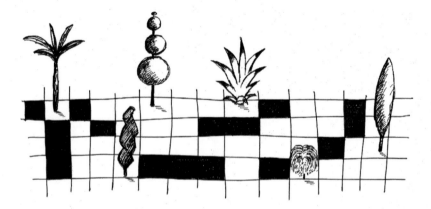

O ver the next rise Sam could see that the line he was following led to a gate made of quills in a sturdy picket fence. *A Trap?* he wondered. *A trick? A net? A catch? A snare?*

Reaching the gate, he saw a sign:

☝☼□♦♦✝□☼♋⚒♒□♋♏ ■♦

Wingdings. Sam frowned.

Underneath, someone had translated the Wingdings:

CRossWoRdGArdenS

What do I do now? I wish Cory was here. He'd know what to do. He always helps me even if he does tease sometimes. Annie, too.

I need some friends.

Sam was even beginning to miss Littlebird.

Hesitating before the gate, he looked for a way around the fence. *Nothing there. No other path in sight. In any direction.*

Finally, with no alternative, he reached out and placed a wingtip on the latch.

Instantly a gatekeeper appeared, seeming to grow right out of the earth. He looked like a penguin. Or even more like a penguin in disguise, dressed in black and white rags. A nametag on his lapel read ALPH. He didn't speak. He just opened the gate, ushered Sam inside, and handed him an envelope with the name SAM on it.

Opening the envelope with his beak, Sam found a message. He took it out carefully, and read:

The groundskeepers welcome you to Crossword Gardens, where some signs are very cross because the words that are stuck on them are mixed up. Some are ordinary baseball terms and some are slang terms. We challenge you to sort out the terms and fit them onto the Crossword Field.

Right in front of Sam was a crossword field with spaces for the letters cut in the grass just like a real crossword puzzle. On the other side of the field was a long row of tall yellow flowers. He read on:

Clues will help you find where the words are supposed to go. When you have solved all the horizontal answers, you will find a hidden vertical message that offers you good advice.

Then compose a letter—here is the letter S. When you are done, there will still be more to do, but when you are finished, the Penguin will let you proceed.

A loose letter S almost fell out. Sam grabbed it and let the note fall to the ground.

Penguin? Slang?

He looked up. The quill-picket fence was still there, but the gatekeeper had disappeared. So had the gate. Sam was penned in.

Then he realized what the message was telling him to do: *"Compose the S and arrange the signs"—that's the first Riddle-task Old Swivelhead said I have to solve before I can get to the park.* So he stepped forward to two signs. The first read:

Okay, those are the words I have to move, Sam thought, ruffling his feathers.

And there's a sign *with something else written on it.*

Next to the word sign was the clue sign. Sam hopped over to it. He read the clue sign five times.

HERE ARE YOUR CLUES.

1. (vertical) PUSH YOURSELF TO DO SOMETHING FASTER (e.g., THROW A BALL)
2. A LEFT-HANDED PLAYER
3. A CURVEBALL
4. A SOFTLY HIT BALL THAT LANDS SAFELY IN THE OUTFIELD
5. A BAT
6. A HARD HIT GROUND BALL
7. RUNNERS ON FIRST, SECOND, AND THIRD
8. A SHARP-EYED BATTER SEES THE BALL THIS WAY
9. WHAT A 4-AND-1 COUNT GETS THE BATTER
10. A QUARREL ON THE FIELD
11. A BROKEN BAT THAT LANDS IN THE INFIELD
12. A HIGH HARD-HIT HOME RUN
13. AN EASY-TO-CATCH HIGH FLY BALL TO THE OUTFIELD
14. THE SHAPE OF THE FIELD
15. THE PLAYERS' BENCH

Sam thought about the clues over and over until he had some idea about how to match the letters in the words with the spaces on the field. The Cross-Word Field. He knew where that was already: right beside him, where spaces had been cut in the grass. Now he just had to peel off the letters and place them in the right spots in the crossword spaces on the field.

But there are fifteen clues and only fourteen words on the word sign. Weird. Numbers don't match up.

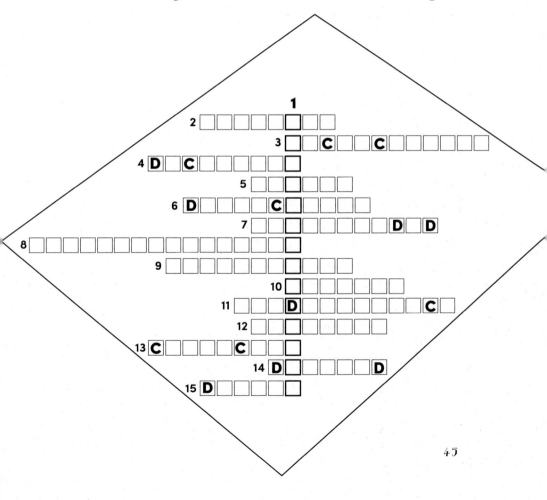

Sam couldn't see any obvious place to put the S, so he dropped it on the uneven ground and set about solving the puzzle as best he could, peeling the letters off the signs and moving them into the right places on the crossword field.

He saw that a few letters were already on the field. *Cs and Ds—that helps, too.*

As he moved the rest of the letters into the puzzle, he laughed at some of the words—especially DUCK SNORT! He felt stronger when he laughed.

Soon he'd filled in every one of the spaces.

The puzzle wasn't all that hard—except for clue number 1. That one's odd. It doesn't make sense.

Picking up the gatekeeper's message, Sam read it once more. This time his eyes stopped on one particular sentence that almost popped out at him.

When you have solved all the horizontal answers, you will find a hidden vertical message that offers you good advice.

"Vertical message," it says. With good advice?

He went back to the clue sign and also read it again, all the way through.

"Vertical," he said aloud. "Vertical." *At the number 1, I have to read vertically.*

So he read down instead of across. And as he did so, the crossword revealed its hidden message.

PUT MUSTARD ON IT.

"That's it?" he protested. "All that work and that's the message?"

It doesn't sound like good advice to me. I don't see how mustard could make me throw better. And how would putting mustard on anything help me solve riddles?

When he looked back at the gatekeeper's letter, different words popped out:

Then compose a letter—here is the letter S. When you are done, there will still be more to do, but when you are finished, the Penguin will let you proceed.

Right, he thought. The riddle has two parts:
"Compose the S, and arrange the signs." *So far I've just done half.*

Sam picked up the letter *S* and stared at it. It didn't say anything. It didn't move. It just sat there. He tried turning it upside down. It looked just the same.

I'm supposed to compose it? How can you compose an S? Sing to it? Draw it? Dip it in mustard? Or maybe—maybe I need to use the S to write for help. But who would I write to? And what can I write with?

He looked around. The quill fence that surrounded CrossWord Gardens ran right behind him, along the edge of the field.

A quill. I can break off a quill and use it to scratch a letter in the dirt. I'll write HELP! And maybe someone flying overhead will see it.

But then he remembered the Raven that the bird voices had talked about. He didn't want any Raven to see him.

Maybe I should write to the Three Owls. They helped me once already. But which one?

If I wrote to Bard, he'd want me to write in rhyme—

> *Dear Bard, I'm*
> *Looking for help,*
> *But nothing rhymes*
> *Except for KELP—*

that won't do. Anyway, Bard's name doesn't start with an S. Neither does Help.

Sam scratched an *S* in the ground. DEAR S, he wrote. *S-who? Which names begin with S? Sam . . . Swallow . . . Sullivan . . . Southpaw?*

It might be Old Swivelhead. But that's an O. Or Snow? Yes—it was Snow who told me I could write for help if I ever needed to!

Sam scratched DEAR SNOW on the ground.

What do I write next? Save me?

Just then a gust of wind shook his feathers, and Sam looked up. Over on the other side of the field, the tall yellow flowers were waving at him.

"Sunflowers!" he exclaimed. *A Burrowing Owl is supposed to be helping me in sunflowers!*

Right away he recalled something else that Old Swivelhead had told him: *Somehow letters* will reveal him to you.

Sam hopped across the field to the sunflowers and looked around. *Those clues were supposed to help me find the One Who's Lost. But I can't see him.*

Sam couldn't even see the Burrowing Owl.

"Where IS the Owl?" he shouted. "And where's the gatekeeper, the one who wears rags?"

No answer.

"And how do I get out of here?"

Still no answer.

"RHUBARB!" Sam bellowed, and he started muttering words that he once heard his Uncle Donovan say. "Dodo dunderloon. Turkey slughead." Somehow they just slipped off the end of his tongue, though they didn't actually seem to mean anything.

Then more of Old Swivelhead's words flitted through Sam's head: "Use your skill with numbers and anagrams. When you think you're done, there's more to do."

Of course. Anagrams. I need to find an anagram—for ANAGRAM?

"I know—it's A RAG MAN!"

Sam flapped his wings and the ragged-patch gatekeeper instantly reappeared. This time the nametag read ABET. A gate opened in the quill fence and Sam walked through. *Why didn't I see it before?* he wondered, looking down at the sandy pathway he was standing on. It beckoned straight ahead. *And where does this go? It looks safe enough. Maybe it will take me to the park. Or Riddle City.*

After taking ten steps along the path, Sam smiled.

Well, that was easy. Compose and Arrange: I've finished my first Riddle-task.

Or have I?

He turned and looked back, but in the time it had taken to swallow once, or maybe twice, the garden, the gate, and the black-and-white gatekeeper—*was it really a penguin?*—had all disappeared.

His smile faded.

• • •

The path forward now looked more dangerous. It started to wind across undulating ground, through long grass and bushes that felt much like a forest, and Sam couldn't see very far ahead.

Naturally. Nothing's straightforward here.

Cautiously he kept going, trying to stay alert, watching on every side for danger. Cats. Or claws. And maybe clues.

All of a sudden a gang of birds sprang out from behind a tree—weaverbirds and purple finches and black-capped chickadees, flapping about in flocks and batches and clutches and bunches, hassling, hectoring, barracking, pestering, all wanting his attention.

Sam wasn't pleased. They didn't sound like friends. "Birdie," pecked one. "Can't fly," pecked another. All Sam could hear was clamour—"Look at MeMeMe, MeMeMe."

Donovan Donovan Sullivan Blake, Sam said to himself. *I don't have to listen to the hassle-birds.*

But I do have to figure out riddles. So what's going on? Is all this noise another riddle? With me in the middle, muddled? I don't understand. What am I missing?

Seeds. The weaverbirds are scattering seeds everywhere—in the grass, on the path—

Sunflower seeds?

It doesn't make sense, but are the weaverbirds somehow helping me with sunflower seeds?

Another clue crossed his mind: *Somehow letters will reveal him to you. If you could grow lettuce, you would see him.*

He dismissed it. The only lettuce Sam had seen was among the crossword clues. *What I really need to know is where the One Who's Lost is. Where's a clue that will tell me that?*

He turned, then tripped over another sign that was almost hidden in the grass.

Have been threatened? Waved the threat?

"They're those same letters. But they still don't make sense," Sam said.

Then he muttered, "Duck Snort!" He picked himself up, laughed out loud, and kept walking.

♦

CHAPTER 5

THE RIDDLEWORLD LEAGUE

The path now started to wind uphill, and the afternoon was getting much warmer. Partway up, Sam started to hear more bird voices: "The Swallow's getting closer . . . Have you seen his Friends? . . . Do they know he's on his way? Shhhh . . . Remember the Raven!"

Where is the sound coming from?

Sam looked up. He saw large numbers of birds gathering near him, and two huge billboards that said T H A N T H W E A V E R and W A R N H A V T E E T H *—what could THEY mean? The weaver has teeth? Or is it another anagram I'm supposed to solve?*

Forget the signs, he told himself sternly.

Ignore the voices, too.

Concentrate.

COUNT the birds: that'll pass the time.

"Pass the time?" he murmured. *That reminds me of something—another Riddle-task? Something Old Swivelhead said: "Use your skill with numbers."*

Okay, I'll do that. Numbers make me focus.

So how many birds can I see? 1, 2—I could count them by ones. Too slow. Or by twos, or by tens, but if I do it this way—

0, 1, 1, 2, 3, 5, 8, 13, 21, 34, 55

—that would be faster. What would the next number be? Oh yes, 89 . . .

Where are all these birds coming from?

When Sam looked ahead he could see a giant figure a kilometre or two away (less than a mile, he calculated). *An object? A giant person? The Careful Giant who's supposed to become my friend?*

He trudged forward, watching on both sides, wary of Ravens and Cats. A bell struck three times: BONG. BONG. BONG. Then silence. Then again it struck: BONG. BONG. BONG.

What's going on?

Soon he could see that the crowd of birds was lining up, and he could hear someone counting them:

Frigatebird ovenbird hoopoe hawk,
Bobwhite bananaquit dotterel auk.

Checking their names? But why?

Joining the back of the line, Sam soon realized that he was the only one who was staying quiet. All the birds in front of him were screeching and squawking. *Complaining to each other—or arguing with the giant?*

As he got closer, he heard more names called out:

Spoonbill razorbill roadrunner wren,
Jackdaw junco yellowlegs hen.

And he could see that the giant figure looked like a clock: a very ornate clock, with cats and butterflies carved all over it. As each bird flew past,

Magpie stonechat gnatcatcher pipit,
Ibis bulbul lorikeet linnet,

the clock ticked: "Foul, Foul, Foul." Loudly.

What on earth is happening this time?

The crowd of birds kept growing:

Wagtail nightingale yellowhammer ruff,
Nightjar goatsucker,

—"NOT CLOSE ENOUGH," struck the clock, adding "Foul, Foul, Foul," until it was almost Sam's turn.

Redstart crossbill marabou murre,
*Wryneck, grosbeak, moa—*NO MORE—

"What do you mean NO MORE?" Sam planted his feet and stood up tall, facing the clock. "Do you mean GO NO FARTHER?"

"I decide. I'm the Umpire Clock. Whatever I decide is my decision." Sam twitched his beak and stood taller still. The clock looked closely at him. Then she changed her tune. "Swallow," she said.

In the same moment, Sam saw that sunflowers had been carved on the clock right among the cats and butterflies. He remembered: "*Somehow letters* will reveal him to you. If you could *grow lettuce*, you could see him. *Swallow etiquette* will take you to him." He still couldn't see the One Who's Lost—or the Burrowing Owl. But guessing at what Old Swivelhead must have meant by the word *etiquette*, he looked back at the clock and said, "Please."

Using her hands, the clock waved Sam on. "Fair," she said. "If you want to get to the outfield, keep driving in the same direction."

Some help that is. The hill's getting steeper. And my legs are getting sore.

Soon birds and birds and more birds than he'd ever dreamed about surrounded Sam. They were hopping on the ground, darting through the trees, flying this way and that, bewilderingly noisy. Sam called out, "Who knows where the baseball park is? I need directions!" *If I hear anything, it will either help me or hinder me. But which is which?*

"The park?" asked a brown-and-green duck. "Are you looking for that, too?"

"Yes," said Sam, turning to see who had spoken.

Then he smiled. He liked how the duck was looking at him. One eye was sort of tilted sideways, as if she were trying to decide whether to stay and talk or get quickly out of the way. "Yes!—and I'm so glad to meet someone I can talk to at last. I'm Sam Swallow, and I didn't always use to be a bird, but since I got to Riddleworld

I've been forever on the road looking for the park so I can play baseball."

"Well I'm Doriana Duck," said the duck, "and I've been told that in the park I'll find the best pond in the world to swim in."

"And I'm Courtland Cassowary the Fourth," said yet another bird, who strode up to them and bent down to talk. This bird was very tall, with black feathers, a red hat, a wattle, and a bright blue neck.

"Courtland?" Sam repeated. "The Fourth?"

"You can call me Cort," he said. "I want to find the park so I can play basketball. I didn't use to look like this. Now I do. I have only three toes, and I can't fly."

"My life changed when my pond dried up," said Doriana, "and I turned into a green-winged teal. I can't fly very well. Not yet anyway. But I'm a dabbler. Which means I can dive if I want to, just not all the time."

Cort added, "And I stretched out when I was offered my favourite food—grapefruit and mustard and a whole can of corn—and I ate too fast."

"You didn't," said Doriana.

"I did," said Cort.

Sam remembered the grapefruit in CrossWord Gardens and pictured Cort swallowing a giant baseball. "Too fast?" he said. "Must have been the mustard."

Doriana eyed him doubtfully, then continued: "I'm serious," she said. "On my way here I met an old owl who told me that I had to help solve a series of tasks before I could find the pond. She said I would need a Giant and a Very Big Smallbird to help me."

"Was it an old Great Horned Owl?" blurted Sam and Cort together—and then Cort told the others what a Great Horned Owl had told him: he, too, could find the park and get out of Riddleworld, but first he'd need to stand up straight and learn his own strength. He'd need a Smallbird to help him, and another who was Smaller than Big but Taller than Short—

"That was confusing. When the owl also said that Riddleworld would teach me to carry things carefully, that confused me even more. In basketball," he protested, "you don't carry, you pass."

Sam didn't ask what he meant. Nor did Doriana. They traded other stories instead. Sam listed the tasks that Old Swivelhead had said he'd have to complete—for 1 2 3 and a 4th to reach home. "There's a song to sing, a maze to escape, a stream to find and cross—and I also have to call out a tongue-untwister, but I don't know how."

"Maybe you'll find out if we all go on together," suggested Doriana. "Let's call ourselves the Riddleworld League. Maybe together we can find what we're looking for. Six eyes are better than two."

"And who knows about toes and webbed feet," Cort added, laughing.

Sam thought again about Old Swivelhead's list, and he smiled. *I composed a letter. Rearranged signs. Solved an anagram. And I have two friends.* He grinned.

They marched off toward the top of the hill, none of them paying much attention to the sign that was nailed to a nearby tree: THREE HAV WANT. But after they reached the top, Sam said, "There's one other thing—one more thing I have to do before I can join a baseball team. Old Swivelhead told me I have to find the One Who's Lost in the middle of Riddleworld, and we haven't got there yet and anyway I don't know where the middle is or even who he is. I just know that he's small and hidden. The old owl gave me some hints, but they don't seem to be working."

The others nodded.

Doriana said, "Maybe we can ask some birds."

Before they could ask, entire flocks of birds broke into an uproar. They were everywhere. On the path, perched in the trees, flapping about in the grass.

"To succeed-seed-seed," shrieked a crane, skittering this way and that, "you have to dance."

"To intercede-seed-seed," screamed a common swift, snatching an insect out of mid-air, "you have to fly."

Cort suddenly started to scratch in the ground for seeds.

"You're not tall enough," moaned a long-faced swan. "You have to be tall to supersede-seed-seed."

"Or short enough."

"Old enough."

"Rough enough."

"Have enough."

"Stuff."

"Stop!" Doriana interrupted.

Cort stood still. But all the other birds just rustled and bustled and warbled and hustled and rattled and tweeted and twittered and peeped. Each had its own advice.

A fidgety robin leapt about, muttering,

"Get the rhythm right,
Get the bright rhythm light,
Hop robin get the worm,
Red robin take a turn,
Hop round, turn about,
Turn left, turn out."

A buzzard scoffed, "Balderdash!"

A ptarmigan clucked, "Gobbleseed!"

A tern snapped, "It isn't your turn."

And a blue-footed booby ignored everyone else and started to dance around Sam, singing:

"RUFFLE my feathers and
SHUFFLE my feet—
Do the BLUE-foot SHUFFLE with
BRIGHT BLUE FEET."

Sam tried to figure out what they were saying, but so many birds were talking at once—"Why are they all dancing?" he groused. "Why are they all saying SEEDS?" *Nobody makes sense. Nothing they say helps. Why is the park so far away?*

My head is spinning, I'm tired of walking, It's hot and my feet hurt and no one's helping me and I'm tired of all . . . this . . .

He flapped one wing in the air.

He was fed up. With everyone and everything, Cort and Doriana included. *The clues aren't working. We aren't moving fast enough. I can't even see the park yet. So what use are clues—and what use are friends when they're not helping me either?*

"What's the name of this place?" Sam called out.

"It's called the Hill of Distraction. Or Contradiction. Or else it isn't," a loon called back.

"Is, too," screamed a jay—"is not—is—isn't."

Sam stamped both his feet and shouted, "RHUBARB! RHUBARB! RHUBARB!"

Cort and Doriana looked at him, then at each other. "But—" said Cort.

"No Buts," Sam flung back.

 An agitated sandpiper darted twitchily about, trying to attract their attention, but Sam was not willing to listen to anything more. Or anyone. The sandpiper went ahead anyway, singing:

jitterbug jitter
  there's a sandpiper near
Do what you can to
  get away from here
Swing behind an oyster
  swoop beneath a clam
Jitterbug jitter
  take a tram take a tram

TAKE A TRAM
  TAKE A TRAM
    Take a tram

I SAID
Jitterbug jitter
  juggle peanut butter jam

TAKE A TRAM
  TAKE A TRAM
    Take a tram

That's all

"All? No way," Doriana said. "That can't be all, or we'd have solved all the old owl's Riddle-tasks already."

"If we even have to," mumbled Sam. He started to blame the Owls. "Bard and Swivelhead gave me the wrong advice." Then he added, "Ignore the birds—they're unimportant." Instantly the sandpiper and all the other birds disappeared, their chatter with them.

"We've been wasting time," Sam continued. "We've never needed these birds. The tasks are too hard. The clues aren't useful, and there's too much to do. There has to be an easier way to get to the park."

Cort and Doriana looked at each other again.

Sam stomped ahead, muttering, "This isn't funny!"

The path had turned rocky, and the trees were covered in dust. There in front of Sam lay a scrap of paper with a garbled message on it:

NAW VAHT THERE

Those letters again. He swerved to face Cort and Doriana.

Despite the afternoon heat, all three of them shivered.

CHAPTER 6

♦

TRAPPED?

Doriana caught up to Sam on the dusty path. "I wonder what's coming next?" she asked, hesitantly. Sam twisted away without answering.

A silky voice broke the awkward silence. "You're coming to see me, of course. I am the one you've always been going to see."

Whoever had spoken was somewhere close by.

Quickly, Cort, Sam, and Doriana all turned to see who it was, almost bumping into a very large, glossy black bird with a sharp beak and glinting red eyes. Sam was certain it hadn't been there before.

The glossy bird smoothed its feathers and looked almost mechanically at each of the three friends. Twice. Once with each eye. Up and down. The bird was extremely large.

"Raven," whispered Cort and Doriana at the same time.

Sam dismissed them, refusing to listen as anger welled up inside him.

Then the bird pinned one of its glinting eyes directly on Sam, and in a gravelly voice, pressed on: "I know where else you'll be going, too." Its voice changed every time it uttered another phrase.

Cort and Doriana ruffled their feathers.

Sam ignored them again. He was fascinated by the large creature, transfixed by its eyes.

Tossing its head, the bird blinked. Then it opened its beak and drawled, "I even already know your name."

"You do?" Sam asked, surprised.

"I do," the bird replied, smoothly. "Just tell it to me and then I'll tell you if I'm correct."

"D-don't," warned Doriana and Cort, stuttering.

"Don't tell me what I can or can't say! I'm not your pet parrot," snapped Sam.

Then he turned back in a rush to answer the jet-black bird. "I'm Sam Swallow, and I need to find

the park where the baseball teams play."

"That's right," crowed the giant bird. "I know this

for a fact because I am Nevar the Marvellous, Ruler of The Roost."

Doriana murmured something, or maybe nothing, just a sound.

"You will have noticed that I can change my voice," Nevar sneered. "That's because I can change anything. I am a Transformer."

"Can you make me taller?" Sam asked.

"With a flick of my wing," Nevar rattled.

"Can you tell me where to find the One Who's Lost?"

"I know exactly where he is. I fly over all of Riddleworld and can even guide you there," Nevar rasped.

"Can you even get me out of Riddleworld and change me into a Byrd City baseball player?" Sam asked.

"I can do anything," Nevar spat. And in a more wheedling voice, he added, "Try me. Go on, try me."

"I—I—," Sam answered, shifting from his left foot to his right.

"There's just one little thing I need you to do for me. It won't hurt you. It will help you. Wouldn't you like that?"

"Yes, but—well—what thing?" Sam stammered.

"All you have to do is tell me where the Burrowing Owl is hiding. He needs my help. All the Owls need my help, even the littlest ones."

"They do?" wondered Sam aloud. *I thought the Burrowing Owl was supposed to be helping me.*

But then Nevar kept talking, his voice getting sharper: "Or you could tell me which of your two friends here you would like me to transform into a statue."

Sam looked at Cort and Doriana. They were standing frozen to the ground, their eyes wide.

"It would be a fine statue and attract a lot of attention in Riddle City. Which one do you choose?"

"Choose?"

But why do I have to choose? Sam thought. *Cort and Doriana are my friends—I think—*

I won't do it.

Not even to be tall.

I just won't do it.

He planted his feet, looked Nevar straight in the eye, and firmly said, "Neither one."

Instantly Nevar opened his beak, twisted a claw, flicked like a switch one corrugated eyelid, let out a gigantic raucous

CAW,

and with a rasping
rattling sound, snatched up all
three of the friends, snapped them
into pockets under his giant wings,
and soared straight up into the air.

It was like flying, but it wasn't flying. Sam couldn't catch his breath. Couldn't speak. Couldn't swallow.

He tried to peer out of the pocket, but he couldn't see anything. He tried to listen, but all he could hear was flap—flap—flap. *Nevar's wings.*

The mechanical sound troubled Sam. *This isn't right. Where is Nevar taking me?*

A moment later: *Where is he taking US?*

And just then he heard Nevar's terrible raw voice taunting him: "KLAW will get you soon—all three of you—when the rooster crows—"

Frightened, Sam realized he needed his friends and wanted to know if they were safe. "Can you hear me, Cort?" he called out, as loudly as he could. "Are you all right, Doriana?"

"Yes, we're all right," they called back. "Are you all right, Sam?"

"Yes. But we need to get out of here. Fast."

But how?

Sam tried to remember all the advice he'd been given. So many things he had to remember in Riddleworld—so many puzzles to solve. He wracked his brain. *There's something I have to do—a maze—a twist—a stream—a climb—*

a rhyme? Maybe it's important that nothing near Nevar rhymes?

"Pass the time and remember to rhyme," Sam suddenly said out loud, and when he did so he felt Nevar's wings lurch a little.

That was the second of the Riddle-tasks—didn't I solve it a long time ago when I was going past the Umpire Clock?

Maybe only half of it. Till now. Maybe I have to solve the rest. Somehow.

Another lurch.

"We have to start rhyming," Sam said to his friends. "That'll make us stop climbing."

Nevar's wings lurched for a third time.

"Did you feel that?" Sam called out.

"Feel what?" asked Cort.

"The lurch. Every time there's a rhyme, Nevar lurches."

"So what do we do?"

"If we're going to get out of here, we have to call out rhymes and work as a team."

"Team Ice cream!" shouted Cort, immediately. "That rhymes. Mealtimes!"

"Still flying . . . Keep trying," said Doriana.

They started to call out random rhymes—"Middle . . . Riddle; Cassowary . . . January; Diver . . . Survivor; Follow . . . Swallow."

They got louder and louder until it was impossible to tell whose voice was whose. "Choose . . . Clues . . . Which ones to Use; We're not trapped in a pocket—We're snapped in . . . unlock it!"

After each rhyme, Nevar-the-Raven tossed and pitched through the sky, jerking back and forth, tumbling closer and closer to the ground.

Cort cheered: "Sam, we'll be free; we're a family of three."

With that, the giant bird shut down. He didn't fall straight from the sky, but he coughed and lost power, his winghold loosening. Juddering and jolting, he slowed and slowed, at last gliding erratically onto a flat field.

The three friends took deep breaths and pried themselves out of Nevar's clutch. His beak was open, but the giant bird said nothing. Both his eyes had clicked shut.

The flat field was covered in yellow sunflowers.

"Which way shall we go?" Cort asked.

"Might not matter," said Sam, looking at a sign that said

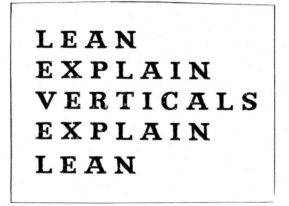

LEAN
EXPLAIN
VERTICALS
EXPLAIN
LEAN

"Does the sign mean we should lean sideways?" asked Doriana.

"Maybe," Sam answered. "But whichever way you read it, forward or backward, it says the same thing—LEVEL. It must mean we're on Level Ground."

"Forward . . . backward," Doriana said. "But the message goes up and down as well. Maybe the ground only looks level because of all the sunflowers."

"They won't be easy to walk through," Cort said, puzzled. "But we can't stay still. We have to keep going."

"Wherever we're going now," Sam said.

"Forward . . . backward," Doriana repeated. "Backward . . . to go forward! Yes. We need to *remember* what to do *next*. That's it."

"Find the One Who's Lost!" Sam cried out. "And figure out who he is."

"I think I have the answer to that," Doriana replied. "The clues were showing us all along who he is, and we just didn't see it."

"What do you mean?" asked Sam and Cort in unison.

"I think it's another letter puzzle, like the one on that LEVEL sign. Think of the first letters in One Who's Lost—they spell out OWL."

"Of course!" exclaimed Sam. "That helps me see where the Burrowing Owl is, too!"

"Is he the One Who's Lost?"

"No, the Burrowing Owl's just hidden—'camou-flaged in sunflowers.' The Burrowing Owl was sup-posed to help me find the One Who's Lost. And he has, but I didn't realize how. I didn't understand I had to read the letters in the word sunfLOWers. What I should have been doing was looking to see how the Burrowing Owl had burrowed into the letters, mixed up his name, and disguised O-W-L as L-O-W."

"Disguised?" asked Cort.

"So that the Cats won't see him, but I will. By looking more closely. To start with," Sam mused, "the letter-disguise might help me remember all the clues Old Swivelhead gave me. I've already remembered some of them—"

*Someh**ow let**ters will reveal him to you.*
*If you could gr**ow let**tuce you could see him.*
*Swal**low et**iquette will take you to him.*

"I still don't understand," said Cort.

"I think I do," interrupted Doriana. "You mean

that Old Swivelhead hid the name of the One Who's Lost inside the letters of the clues."

"Exactly," said Sam. And slowly he recited Old Swivelhead's remaining clues:

*Cross yell**ow** lines if you would seek him.*
 *Narr**ow**-leaved vines will almost hold him.*
 *Wind**owl**ight will nearly reach him.*
Stay on the ground and you will miss him.
Rope and cage do not contain him.

"Maybe 'cross yellow lines' means we have to cross through this yellow sunflower field," Cort suggested.

"And we probably have to look for a place with windows and vines," said Doriana.

"But first we have to know for sure *who* we're looking for," Sam stressed. "Most of the clues hide the letters O-W-L and O-W-L-E-T. I think the One Who's Lost has to be OWLET, the little Saw-whet Owl who was missing from the signpost when I first met Old Swivelhead, and Bard, and Snow."

"OWLET?" Cort asked.

"Saw-whet?" Doriana asked. "You mean *whet*, like *sharpen*?"

"Yes," Sam answered. "Owlet's his name. And he's a Saw-whet Owl because his call sounds something like *skiew*—like the sharpening of a saw. That has to be who he is. But where is he?"

"Maybe over there," said Cort, standing up tall and looking across the tops of the plants. He pointed toward the horizon. "I think I can see something far off. Maybe it's the Middle of Riddleworld."

In the distance the three friends heard a band playing.

"Let's follow the music," said Doriana. "At least we know who we're looking for now. All we have to do is find him."

"Simple," said Sam.

The wind picked up then, and afternoon clouds began to build along the horizon. Heading off through the yellow field, the three friends didn't look back to see if Nevar had begun to move.

CHAPTER 7

♦

The Tower in Riddle City

Picking their way through sunflowers, the three friends stumbled onto a grassy path.

Standing on tiptoes, Cort told the others: "I can see the towers of a city ahead. There's a wall around the outside, and a gigantic sign above the entrance gate, with flashing lights that spell out COME TO RIDDLE CITY, YOU'LL BE AMAZED."

The friends stepped forward cautiously. Words in Riddleworld could mean anything.

As they drew nearer, a new sign said,

WELCOME
KEEP OFF THE GRASS

But by the time they reached it, the path had grown dustier, and there wasn't any grass.

"Rubble and bricks," Sam muttered. "Trouble and tricks." He was on the lookout for danger.

Just outside the entrance gate, four large catbird statues, each with its feet in a milky pool, rose up in front of them. A fifth statue, the largest one, looked like a hungry pterodactyl. **FILIGREE FINGERWING**, said its label.

"A Lizard-bird?" Sam wondered aloud, carefully inching past. "Must be one of Klaw's mechanical tricks."

Sam, Cort, and Doriana slipped through the gate. The band was playing, and the music was louder.

"Which street should we follow?" Cort asked.

A sign appeared right in front of them:

YOU MIGHT WISH TO FOLLOW THE ARROWS

but right after this one, they saw another, which read:

OR YOU MIGHT WISH NOT TO

"What does that mean?" Cort asked.

Sam laughed. "The arrows are pointless."

In the shadows just ahead, they nearly tripped

into a well, and Sam again tried to laugh at their predicament. "These roads are not well marked."

"We're being warned, not welcomed," Doriana said, sombrely.

The three friends looked around and again wondered which way to go. Streets led off in all directions, some crooked, some looped, some circling back on themselves, some stopping at dead ends.

As evening approached, less and less light filtered down. Shapes loomed up. They thought they saw cats everywhere. Even simple shadows appeared threatening.

"Now is not the time to slow down," said Doriana. "We have to FIND Owlet."

"Where?" asked Cort.

"Old Swivelhead mentioned a maze," Doriana said.

"This entire city is a maze," Cort said.

Enter the maze and escape it again, the third Riddle-task, thought Sam.

"And didn't a clue say we'd miss Owlet if we stayed on the ground?" Doriana continued. "Might Owlet be lost in a tower? Perched in a tree?"

"The Tower of Klaw," Sam said, remembering. "The whispering bird voices mentioned Klaw's Tower. We have to find that. Let's keep following the music. And walk faster."

Put mustard on it, he told himself.

They searched a long time before discovering who was playing the music.

When they walked down one street, they seemed closer to it, but when they turned into the next, the sound seemed farther away.

After several tries, they finally stumbled into a large square. On all four corners, blues bands were talking to each other through the music they were playing. A trumpeter swan on one corner, a song sparrow on another, a banded flicker strumming a guitar.

When the friends asked, "Where is the nearest tower?" all they got for an answer was more music. A stork plucked a bass, an emu coaxed a clarinet, a parrot blasted a saxophone, a quail wailed, a puffin bellowed, an oriole rapped on a yellow snare drum.

They strode quickly around each of the first three corners, but when they got to the fourth, Sam was so caught up in the mesmerizing rhythm that he wanted simply to stay on the street, swing to the beat—remembering only just in time to ask in the loudest, politest voice he could muster, "WHERE IS THE TOWER? PLEASE."

With a flick of his drumstick, the drummer said, "You're right beside it. You're almost in it. You'll find the inning. In a minute."

Sam looked up. A tall box-like structure, half covered in narrow leaves, stood at the edge of the square.

"Why didn't one of us notice that?" Cort asked.

"We weren't looking," Doriana answered.

She went closer to the box tower, and after walking around it once and staring up at it carefully, she started asking questions. "Why does this tower have no door? Is there a secret way in? It looks as though it would be a good hiding place. This must be Klaw's base."

"It's covered in vines," Sam said aloud. "Narrow-leaved vines will almost hold him."

"There seems to be something up there, partway up."

She leaped and stretched and flapped her wings. "But I can't make out what it is."

"I can, though," Cort replied. "I can jump." Cort leaped up as high as he could. "There's nothing much to see. There's no door-knocker, no bell, no buzzer, no window, no door-handle of any sort. The wall is absolutely plain, except—well—at one place you can see an outline of what looks like a door, and all around its edge are scratch marks."

"But that's it," said Doriana, brightening.

"What's it?"

"The entrance. The Oriole just told us we'd find the way in. Jump up again and push at the claw-marked door shape—maybe it's actually Klaw-marked."

Cort jumped up, and as he did, Doriana called out, "And shout out OWLET!"

Cort did that, but nothing happened. "What next?" he asked.

"There has to be a password," Sam said. "The Owls said that Owlet had to be *called back*—so maybe we can imitate his call—*SKIEW!* Quickly now, jump again! And this time carry me with you!"

Cort picked up Sam and, holding him tight, he jumped, pushed at the clawed outline around the door, and called out *"SKIEW!"*

When nothing happened, he jumped and called again: *"SKIEW!"*

On the third try, a door to the tower creaked slowly inward. Sam couldn't see very far inside, but Cort clamped one of his three-toed claws onto the leafy vine, holding on until both he and Sam could step through the doorway.

They found themselves in a dark, tight passage littered with sawdust. It smelled like sour milk.

Shuffling across the floor to the far end of the passage, Sam spied a staircase that led upwards into an even darker dark. Raven beaks and cat claws projected out of the wall and into the stairwell. Shivers ran up and down his spine.

"Don't be a mouse," Cort said firmly, standing up straight. He took one step, then two, then three and four.

Sam followed him into the heart of the tower.

"Hurry!" Doriana shouted from down below. "Remember Nevar. Danger's going to strike when the rooster crows."

"But it's almost nightfall. Roosters crow at dawn," Cort said.

"It won't be dawn when the Riddleworld Rooster starts to crow," Sam explained. "It'll be nightfall. Everything here is turned around."

Warily, Cort and Sam climbed. The staircase circled higher and higher, and with every step they took, the tower hissed, the ceiling got lower.

Sharp talons burst abruptly out of the wall whenever Sam felt afraid. "Donovan," he whispered. "Donovan. Sullivan. Blake."

Partway up the stairs, the ceiling suddenly closed in, and Sam saw Cort crouch down because he was so tall. A key was dangling from a talon. When Cort stopped to grab it, Sam sped ahead of him, hurrying round and around till finally he reached a long narrow attic at the top of the tower. It was silent, but not empty. It stank of mould and decay.

Dim windowlight filtered in through slits in the roof. To Sam the room looked like a giant coop. Birdcages lined the walls, latches held each cage closed, and shapes were curled up inside them all.

Every one of these shapes looks like a corkscrew. Or a pretzel. Except— all the shapes in the cages have heads and feet!

Some looked like metal finches. Some like melted chickadees. Some looked like gulls. One looked like a plastic flamingo.

A last ray of sunshine cast pale light onto the floor, and in the circle of light—Sam stopped beside one cage—the shape in the cage looked like a tiny owl. Its feet were tied with rope and attached to an iron ring in the floor. Its wings were clipped. Its mouth was wrenched to the side. But its eyes were wild, racing—

"Owlet?" Sam asked.

Only twisted sounds came out of the small owl's mouth—but the eyes were flicking back and forth and up and down.

"What on earth . . . ?" Cort stumbled into the room. "Unriddle this place, Sam, or I will . . ."

Remembering the fourth Riddle-task, Sam called out, "Skiew, Skiew, Skiew! A tongue-untwister to break the chains!"

The iron ring immediately broke and the small lost owl struggled to speak. "WHO am I?"

"You're—" Sam began, and then whispered, "You're family."

Sam quickly loosened the ropes that held Owlet fast. At the same time, without thinking about what he was doing, he started to sing:

If you ever hear a falcon
In the furrow of a sigh,
Just sing little kookaburra songs,
You are strong—

Instantly, the whole tower shook. The cages and the metal shackles that were pinning the shapes inside the cages disintegrated.

The Riddleworld Rooster started to crow.

A raven screamed: CAW—AW–AW–AW*wwww*

A cat screeched: ME**RROUUW**WwWE**R**RR**ʀ**

And then a great sound of rustling filled the room as all the twisted shapes turned back into birds and regained their colourful feathers.

And found their voices.

"What's going on?" Cort called.

"We've untwisted their tongues," Sam replied. "And I've found Owlet. So I've completed Riddle-task Four—and maybe even Five. Because for some reason I started singing. Now let's get out of here—we have to leave the City. That's the solution to the second half of Riddle-task Three."

"Catch on to the feathers on my back—I'll carry you down," said Cort. "Owlet, you jump on, too," he added. "I'll be careful."

The tower itself was starting to crack. The roof was chipping and splitting. Bits of ceiling were smashing to the floor.

Cort dodged and swerved as the room closed in on them.

So many birds were now stretching their feathers—lyrebirds, peacocks, pelicans, cranes—and so many

spreading their wings
wide—geese and gulls and
galahs—that they bumped into each other as
they rushed all together toward the narrow exit, Sam
and Cort and Owlet among them. Whooping, shriek-
ing, screaming, squawking, they clambered out of the
room into the dark stairway. Down they raced, down
and down, the staircase hissing as the walls shivered
and rumbled, and holes opened below them.

Massed together, large and small—emus, pink
flamingos, albatrosses, larks—the cramped birds
lurched every time a wall heaved. They knocked
against each other when they missed a step. They
slipped, they slid, they tripped and skidded. Their
claws lost their grip on the unstable stairs, and
down they fled—sprinting, scrambling, rushing,
dashing—down through the buffeting
dark as fast as they could, away
from the tower room.
The walls closed
in. The low ceiling
broke into shards.

Crashes and clatter erupted behind them, the Cat's cry echoing at every turn. Flailing and whirling, jostling and pitching, they raced forward, a flurry of feathers spinning toward a glimmer of light that shone ahead of them, till they reached the tower door, still high off the ground, and leaped without hesitation into open air.

Those that could fly, flew. Those that could hop and clamber, hopped and clambered down the narrow-leaved vine. Cort jumped, with Sam on his back, still holding on to Owlet, hanging on to the end of the rope that had been tied to Owlet's legs.

Doriana was waiting for them.

"Run," Cort panted. "Fast—we have to work our way out of here."

"Klaw might still find us, and maybe Nevar-the-Raven, too," Sam shouted.

Away they ran, across the square, avoiding stones and sticks as best they could, turning without thinking into the first street they saw. By the time they stopped, it was night. Sam couldn't remember how many corners they'd run past or gone around. They were deep in the Maze.

CHAPTER 8

◆

THE MAZE

"The streets are so dark now," Doriana panted. "How will we get out of the city, especially when we don't know where we are?"

"I can help," Owlet answered in a quiet small voice. "I can see in the dark."

But the streets confused them. Alleys and lanes and roundabouts kept leading them astray. They had to avoid a booby trap, a cage with doors that snapped shut, a swampy ditch, an electric snare. Once they found themselves in a corridor of mirrors, where Sam lost track of what was real and what was just a reflection. The flap-flap-flapping of Nevar's wings started up again, overhead.

"Don't get distracted," Sam urged. "If we can get to the city wall, we can follow the wall to the exit gate."

Cort held out the key that he'd found in the tower.

"Maybe it will open the gate," he said.

"Keep it safe," Sam said. "But keep it handy, in case we need it quickly."

They wound their way forward.

At last they reached the city's brick wall (10 metres high, Sam guessed: 32.8 feet). Pitted with pigeonholes, it stretched ahead. A series of locks marked regular distances. Cort tried his key in the first—then the next and the next. Every lock refused to budge.

Several times the friends nearly tumbled, but every time when they regained their balance, Cort checked to see that he had the key tucked safely away.

Soon they encountered a sign that read:

SOMETIMES YOU MUST GO BACK TO GO FORWARD

"To look for what?" Doriana asked, then continued, "I wonder. Maybe it's something that will help you with a riddle, Sam. What's the next one you have to solve?"

"'Break the ice to catch the tram,'" answered Sam. "I don't understand what that means."

"Perhaps all those other signs we passed will help," Doriana suggested. "Do you remember them? If we can put them in some sort of order, maybe they'll tell us something."

"One said THREE HAV WANT," said Cort.

"And there was one that bothered us all," added Doriana. "NAW VAHT THERE. We shivered when we saw that."

"The ones that I walked past," Sam said, "didn't make any sense: THAN TH WEAVER, TH WEATH-ERVAN, WHAV THREATEN, whatever that means— and one near the Umpire Clock: WARN HAV TEETH. Another was in bits when I first arrived in Riddleworld."

Owlet stirred.

"I suppose it could be code," mused Doriana.

"The signs all use the same letters—do you think someone is trying to tell us something," Sam responded, "but isn't able, or isn't allowed, to say it aloud?"

Cort laughed. "Well, if you rearrange the letters you get HAH, WART EVENT."

Doriana gave him a look.

"Or NEVAR WHET HAT," she said, quietly.

Flap—flap—flap overhead.

"Or—or"—Sam didn't want to say what he was thinking—"THAW THE RAVEN."

All four of them flinched.

"DON'T GIVE AN INCH," Cort said loudly. His voice echoed.

Sam thought Nevar would hear. "Hide!" he whispered.

They crowded into a brick-lined alcove, avoiding a faucet that had been fixed into a side wall, with the word *WARM* displayed prominently above it. Sam noticed that all the bricks in the alcove were marked with a check except one on the back wall—

On that wall someone had scrawled a message:

FREE THE UNBLAZED BRICK.

Flap—flap—flap.

Cort bent into the alcove, tucked his legs up underneath his beak, and leaned back hard against the back wall. The plain brick behind him suddenly gave way, and the whole wall collapsed.

Behind the wall was a well.

Sam heard a splash.

"The key," Cort gasped. "I've dropped the key!"

He looked at Sam. Sam looked back.

"Don't panic," said Doriana. "Remember, I can swim. I can dive, too, if I choose. I'll dive down and pick the key up."

As quick as a splash she had the key in her bill.

"But how will we get Doriana out of the well?" Cort asked Sam.

"You and I will lower Owlet's rope to her, and we'll pull her back up. Or we'll find a bucket."

Doriana snorted. "I can fly out," she called, awkwardly, still holding the key in her bill. "I haven't tried flying for a while, but I think I can."

She flapped her wings and soon lifted out of the water. When she reached the alcove, she gave Cort back the key and turned to Sam.

"Sam, I saw something else down there," she said. "On a ledge, just above the waterline—a large square block of what looks like ice. A creature of some sort is frozen inside it—we can't leave it there."

"What can we do?" Cort asked.

"Use the rope, Sam. Give me one end of it," Doriana said.

Of course! Sam handed it to her, and after she flew back down with it into the well, Sam heard a great heave and rustle.

Then he and Cort pulled on the rope, with Owlet urging them on, till slowly the block of ice reached the surface and lay on the alcove floor.

When all four friends had caught their breath and Doriana had flapped her wings three times, they looked more closely at the creature inside the ice—

and jerked back, stunned.

It was a Raven.

Cort was preparing to push the block back down the hole when Sam called out, "Wait!" He had noticed some writing etched into the ice—from the inside. It looked almost unreadable:

CREALBIRDOLD

"Another puzzle," Sam said.

"Another? How do we solve this one, then?" asked Cort.

Owlet answered, speaking quietly. "First you need to solve the message on the wall."

"What message?" asked Doriana.

"It said FREE THE UNBLAZED BRICK," Cort murmured. "But it broke when the wall fell. Is it maybe another anagram, Sam? It uses the same letters as UNFREEZE THE BLACK BIRD! But—"

"No Buts," said Sam. "You're right." Then, "Look!" he whooped. "All the messages are related! The inscription in the block of ice says:

CREALBIRDOLD

or if you write it a different way, it says:

C (real bird) OLD."

"You see, the COLD holds the REAL BIRD. And remember what all those coded signs were telling us to do? THAW THE RAVEN? They must have meant a Real Raven. This one. The one that we're supposed to unfreeze!"

"That other Raven—Nevar, the one who works for Klaw—was obviously an impostor. This bird has to be the real Raven. Riddle-task Seven said 'break the ice to catch the tram'—so we have to free the Raven from the ice before Nevar sees what we're doing."

Nevar's flap-flap-flapping came closer.

Cort, Sam, and Owlet frantically pecked with their beaks and scratched with their claws, trying to break through the ice. Tiny chips fell onto the ground. Nothing else. The scratching had almost no effect.

"You'll take forever if you just keep battering the ice that way," Doriana said, impatiently.

"So what's your solution?" Sam asked.

The flap-flap-flapping came even closer.

"We can melt the ice with warm water," she said, stepping over to the faucet on the wall and turning it on. Sam had forgotten it was there. He was about to say "Good Idea," when hot water cascaded full blast onto the floor of the alcove. The friends leaped out of the way, shouting, "Careful!" "Watch it!" "Look out!" "Turn it down!" "Stop!"

Nevar's flap-flap-flapping sounded louder still.

Desperately they all pushed the block of ice under the faucet. Water gushed over it. Fissures opened, gradually, and then more and more quickly the ice melted. The real Raven stepped free, glistening and black.

The bird cawed once, clearly and sharply. As soon as he did, the sound of mechanical flapping wings abruptly stopped.

The real Raven turned and said, "Thank you. My name is Corbin-the-Dark. I was locked in the ice ten years ago by the creature whose real name is Nevar-the-Cold."

The four friends shuddered.

"You need not fear Nevar any more," he continued, "at least as long as you remain in Riddle City. For a while—but not necessarily forever—his strength has been taken from him, and strength of a different kind has been given to each of you to use as you will. Now that you have freed me, it is in my power to free you from all the traps in the Maze—BUT—"

Sam wanted to say "No Buts"—this time he knew enough to hold his tongue.

"BUT," continued Corbin-the-Dark, looking directly at Sam, "when you leave Riddle City you will be in the Eagle's territory, not mine. And you will have to meet him on your own. If you ask the right question, all will be well. Your friends will be with you, but they will also not be with you. And that is all I am allowed to say."

Sam had heard some of this before, but it had seemed clearer then.

"To leave Riddle City you must remember the sandpiper. When you do, you will find yourselves almost where you want to be."

Sam tried to remember what the sandpiper had said to them just before they'd left the Hill of Distraction. He frowned. *Why isn't it clear?* Then he broke into a laugh. "Oh—I know. She said, 'Take a tram take a tram take a tram.'"

"TRAM," said Owlet. "Rhymes with Sam."

Sam looked at him. He could have sworn Owlet was smiling.

Corbin dipped one wing.

A tram appeared out of nowhere, screeched to a halt beside the four friends, and two conductors stepped onto a platform.

"I've seen them before somewhere," Sam said to the others. "They remind me of Bard and Snow. And the ragman Penguin. Maybe it's their black-and-white suits."

Cort turned around, swiftly. "You could be spotting a trick," he remarked.

"Or a mirror image," Doriana said, reflectively.

The conductors' lapels blinked on and off:

this tram arrives only when required
this tram runs only when desired
this tram leaves after gaining speed
no tickets needed

"Now that he's been found, Owlet will return home to his post in the North," said Corbin. "The conductors will take him there."

Home, thought Sam.

"At least the homes in Riddle City are safe, now that Klaw's been defeated," he said to Cort and Doriana. "The birds can rebuild the statue of the Admirable Bird, too."

"But we never actually saw Klaw. Maybe he's just hiding in the bushes," said Doriana.

"I'm wondering now if anyone has ever really seen Klaw," Sam mused, "or if he only shows up when they're afraid."

Sam took a deep breath. Cort stood up straight. Doriana stretched a wing. Owlet fidgeted. The conductors checked their watches.

Corbin intervened. "Are you getting on the tram or not?"

"Yes!"

Stepping aboard, the travellers waved to Corbin, who waved one wing back.

As the tram started to move, Cort turned to Sam. "Has another Riddle-task been solved?"

"More than one," Sam answered. "We've found the tram and Owlet's going home, so that finishes Riddle-task Seven and Riddle-task Six. And we're just about to get out of the Maze, so at last that's Riddle-task Three as well."

"What that means . . ." Doriana started to speak—

". . . is that Riddle-task Eight, 'crossing the stream,' has to be close," Sam interjected.

He broke off. *Which will leave only Nine and Ten: meeting the Eagle and counting down to one. I'll be able to do those on my own.*

· · ·

In no time, the tram carried everyone safely to the Riddle City gate and stopped to let Cort, Sam, and Doriana step off. As soon as they'd said good-bye to Owlet and the conductors, the tram disappeared.

The three friends looked up at the gate. It was very high.

"My turn," said Cort, taking out the key he'd been carrying. This time it fit directly into the lock, shone silver, and opened the gate smoothly.

No crashing. No squeaking. No slamming. No creaking.

Rhymes are still near, I hear. They've been looking out for us all along.

As they left the city, the darkness died away. Outside the gate, in the sunshine, the three friends smiled.

But there's always something more to do in Riddleworld.

Isn't there?

CHAPTER 9

♦

RIDDLEWORLD PARK

Outside the city wall, the friends saw the park stretch ahead.

Green space. Trees. A basketball court. A pond.

In a far corner was the baseball diamond.

At last!

A wide, fast, very deep stream wound between them and the near edge of the park.

"It's Riddle-task Eight!" Sam declared. "'Find a stream and cross it cleverly.' The key to the puzzle has to be in the word *cross*—because it can mean *go across* and it can also mean *make an X*. And we're at the *EX*treme edge of Riddleworld."

"My feet make *W*s in the sand," said Cort, looking down.

That gives me an idea, Sam thought, and he traced the word *STREAM* into the sand.

"What are you doing?" Doriana protested.

Then Sam scratched a giant *X* over the top of the word *STREAM*, crossing it out.

As soon as he'd done so, the whole landscape

changed. The wide deep stream that had run between them and the park became an *EX-STREAM*.

"Oh!" said Doriana. "Now I see. That *was* clever!"

"Out-*standing!*" Cort echoed.

The friends stood still, staring quietly at the bluegrass that now grew where the stream had once flowed. The park unrolled before them. The court, the pond, and the baseball diamond all looked reachable at last.

Nothing stood in their way.

Sam stirred. He realized that from here on he would have to travel alone.

Each of us will.

But he lingered, not wanting yet to say good-bye.

"Did you know that my name means 'the ocean?'" Doriana asked.

"Everyone's name means something," Cort said.

"I wonder what my name means," said Sam. "I wonder if I can really join a baseball team. I wonder if—"

"Stop wondering," the other two said. "Go join your team. But remember us."

"Always," said Sam. Then he kept talking. "If we ever get home, and even if Byrd City turns out to be more of a riddle than this place is, let's meet at the edge of the park, and talk about the Riddleworld League."

They all agreed. Then Cort laughed. "Will we recognize each other?"

"I hope so," said Sam.

"And Sam," said Cort, "Doriana and I will come and watch you play baseball."

So away they walked to their separate parts of the park—Cort to the east, Sam to the west, Doriana to the south—looking back from time to time and waving till they were out of sight.

Sam imagined Doriana diving deep into the pond, and Cort jumping as high as the hoop. He was happy for them both.

He was also tired. Tired, nervous, excited. And alone.

As he moved toward the baseball diamond, Sam stretched his wings. Getting closer, he saw young weaverbirds flying about everywhere—and grackles, tanagers, sandpipers, thrashers, sparrow hawks, gooney birds, goldfinches, loons—all in brightly coloured uniforms, with names emblazoned on their shirts that said, "Blue Jays" or "Orioles" or "Cardinals."

It feels a little like the Hill of Distraction. Or not.

But I'm here. The tryouts are starting! Nothing is going to stop me now. Not even a penguin.

When he saw the bases on the field, he started to run faster and faster till it felt like flying. *Put mustard on it.*

He could see the coach now, too, a powerfully built bird with fierce eyes and a startling curved beak.

As soon as Sam got close enough, he ran up to him and all in one breath asked, "My-name's-Sam-Swallow-can-I-try-out-for-the-team?"

"Of course you can, son. My name's Eaglehart, but you can call me Coach from now on. And you're so tall I think we'll try you out at shortstop. How does that sound?"

It sounded great to Sam.

Riddle-task Nine, he thought.

And he laughed out loud.

Then almost right away he lost track of time, for suddenly he was on a team, along with several other birds who'd apparently never played together before. Coach was organizing practice drills and rapid-fire relays. And then it was time to play other teams. Whole games went by so quickly that all Sam was sure of was that his team kept losing. They dropped balls and struck out and got caught off base, and rival teams played so much better. But Coach kept them practising. Every one of them got stronger and faster, and soon they started to have fun—and win games together—and then play-offs—

Before you could say *Roar Roar Riddleworld*, it was the day of the League championship, last inning.

Sam was at bat, the win in the balance.

The Ravens' pitcher's really good, thought Sam. *And he's left-handed.*

A wicked curveball. *Uncle Charlie.*

He swung and missed.

"Strike," called the umpire.

Then a second curveball.

"Strike Two."

Sam pulled himself back together.

Focus!

All of a sudden, coming toward him, was the fiercest fastball he'd ever seen.

Sam watched it and watched it and—swung the bat as hard as he could—and hit into just fair territory in the far right corner of the field—a single—*DUCK SNORT?—no, a double, I can do it—*

Then a throwing error—the ball missed Second, and Coach was urging Sam on, and then on again, spinning round Third and down the line—

Pandemonium—

Sam was concentrating so hard on touching the plate that at first he scarcely heard any of the revelry in the stands—"Way to go, Bird!" the crowd was cheering and chanting—though while he was running, he thought he did hear:

TEN nine strange birds,
Then there were eight—
First base Second base,
Circulate—
Seven six five four
Three two ONE—
Home plate anyone,
          anyone,
                    anyone—

Voices—so many—

Till everything got even more confusing. He was sliding—wasn't he? *So much noise.* Hearing voices, fragments of voices, saying "Who—Who—" familiar—*a lot like my mother and dad*—breathless, asking—Who—And counting—*TWO—one TWO—five FOUR three two one—SAFE*!

Sam opened his eyes. He was lying in the dust at the foot of the steps that led up to his back deck.

At home? But when? How?

"Are you all right?" someone asked.

"Do you know—who I am?" someone else was asking.

"Can you touch your nose?"

What weird questions. Sam lifted a wing—no, an arm—I have my hands and feet back?—nose, too?—No beak? No feathers anymore?

What on earth?

"Is it still TODAY?" Sam blurted.

CHAPTER 10

◆

HOME

Late in the summer—weeks later—Sam was walking back to his house. Byrd City Park was not as far away as he used to think it was. His blue and gold uniform said EAGLES on the front and SWALLOW on the back, along with the number 6.

He was smiling, thinking about the home run he'd just hit. *My first ever—in the best game ever!*

"SamMEE!" the crowd had chanted. "SamMEE!"

He'd remembered Cort's words—"Everyone's name means something." Adding, *The trick is to make it matter.*

Though it wasn't easy being Sammy. *Everything was so confusing in Riddleworld—when the world turned upside down. And now?*

That day when Sam had raced out the door, flown through the air, and ended up landing in the dust at the bottom of the stairs, he didn't get to the tryouts. He'd wanted to go. But they wouldn't let him, at least not right away.

When they'd first asked if he felt all right, he started talking about Riddleworld, about wings and claws and the bird-tongue he'd had to use in order to speak with a Cassowary, Four Owls, a Duck. *And Both Ravens.* Everyone just smiled. "Oh yes?" they said. Then they asked if his head hurt.

"I feel stretched," Sam had answered, "but unscratched. Nothing catastrophic."

He didn't get to the park till the next afternoon. The tryouts were held over, and that's when Coach had sized him up and said, "So you're Sam"—as though he knew he was coming, somehow.

He said SAM. Sam liked him already.

"Can you catch?" Coach had asked. "Can you run and slide?" *And I said YES and YES.*

"Well let's see how fast you can fly around the bases."

So I showed everyone—
All that practice paid off—
I'm glad I wasn't alone, though.

Sam was named to the Eagles, one of the Byrd City Park teams, along with the Weaver twins, it turned out, and a lot of the other kids from his school—*Finch and Piper, Swannie and Jay,*

Burrows and Kes and Robin and Bill—Sam could name them all now.

But then he had to learn a lot more.

What to do, when to do it. And how.

Practice, practice, more practice (a catch-and-throw move that Coach calls "the Crow-hop"). Watching the ball ("Think of it as a Grapefruit," Coach says). Base-running ("Move! You're not a Statue!"). Fielding ("Stop stopping to Pick the Daisies!").

Once, when Sam was tossing the ball to First, he almost laughed out loud when Coach shouted, "Put some Mustard on it, Swallow!"

Working as a team was harder to learn ("I told you: No Rhubarbs!").

Coach helped in all kinds of ways.

Like today, thought Sam.

Today they'd been playing the Wildcats, who were really strong, leading the League, and before the game, Coach had reminded the whole team that they were Eagles now.

"Therefore," Coach said, "you have to *be* eagles. You need to breathe in, really deep, and create a force field around yourselves so that nothing can distract you—no sound, no threat, no mask, no trick, no hassle, no catcall, no hubbub, not even a cheer. Remember the eagle."

born in the fir tops
bald eagle embraces air
scaling higher still

"Think what you'll be looking at,"

stillness—illusion:
the eagle's eye notices
one steelhead rising

"And think what you'll be listening for,"

inaudible sound:
air under the eagle's wing
holding still, rushing

"Understand?"

Sometimes Coach is hard to understand, Sam thought. *But I've learned a lot since I started playing.*

The important thing is that I know who I am.

Am I the same Sam as I used to be? Not exactly. I've changed in a lot of ways. Maybe ten. Maybe more.

He didn't stop to count. Not even by fours.

Twice on the way home Sam heard flap—flap— flap overhead, and taken aback, he glanced at the sky. The first time, the sound came from a flag on the end of a flagpole, fluttering and flopping, back and forth. The next time he saw a kite caught in tree branches, flailing away in the summer breeze, as tangled up as a stubborn riddle.

"But easier to explain," Sam laughed, looping his glove around the end of his bat and shouldering it.

He turned the cap on his head around. He tossed a baseball up in the air and caught it when it came back down. Before long he was back home at the end of the tram line.

It looks the same as it always does.

They were sitting on the deck under a sun umbrella—father, mother, uncle Donovan—drinking lemonade and filling in the crossword puzzle in *The Daily Rime.*

His father was whistling. The parrot was squawking.

A pitcher of flowers stood on a table.

An owl-shaped weathervane turned slowly on top of the post in the vegetable garden. And Clio the cat was lying in the shade of a laurel bush, watching a swallowtail butterfly flutter into the sunflowers above her head, out of reach. Then she stretched, licked one paw as though that was the only reason she'd needed to wake up at all, and curled back to sleep.

Sam looked at his watch. It said five minutes to five.

"Hi, sport," said Uncle Donovan cheerfully, "want to see a trick?"

"Maybe tomorrow," answered Sam. *I've seen enough tricks for now.*

"Hello, dear," said his mother, looking over the top of her clear round glasses, "you've been out all afternoon. Did you have fun?"

"I hit a home run. And I made some new friends."

His father looked up. Smiling, he said, "Good for you. I think you've grown, son. And do you know what else happened today? Cory found the key to the front door—it was hanging on a hook under the attic stairs. And I fixed the back door—so it doesn't slam any more."

"Doesn't slam," said Parker the parrot. "Doesn't slam."

Cory and Annie suddenly burst into the yard, talking loudly over top of each other: "Great game . . . we saw you play . . . did you see us? . . . you were terrific . . . did you hear us cheering? . . . you're the best shortstop ever . . . want to go swimming later? . . . or shoot some hoops? . . . we've been looking for you . . . everywhere . . . *Eagles rule!*"

Sam looked at them both. He smiled and nodded. "With you in a minute."

I have some old friends, he thought. *Swallows rule, too.*

Then Littlebird toddled over from where he'd been playing. He reached out his arms.

"Hi, Ollie," said Sam, picking him up and whispering in his ear, "one day I'll teach you how to play baseball."

Overhead, a raven dipped one wing, and high above, an eagle soared on currents of air.

Ollie smiled, and gurgled. "Bam."

Sam laughed.

"Rhymes with Sam," he said.